AM I YOURS?

Alex Latimer

OXFORD
UNIVERSITY PRESS

Great Clarendon Street, Oxford OX2 6DP

Oxford University Press is a department of the University of Oxford.
It furthers the University's objective of excellence in research, scholarship,
and education by publishing worldwide. Oxford is a registered trade mark of
Oxford University Press in the UK and in certain other countries

Text and illustration copyright © Alex Latimer 2018

The moral rights of the author and artist have been asserted

Database right Oxford University Press (maker)

First published 2018

British Library Cataloguing in Publication Data available

ISBN: 978-0-19-275946-7

1 3 5 7 9 10 8 6 4 2

Printed in China

Paper used in the production of this book is a natural, recyclable product made
from wood grown in sustainable forests. The manufacturing process conforms
to the environmental regulations of the country of origin

AM I YOURS?

Alex Latimer

OXFORD
UNIVERSITY PRESS

Two hundred million years ago
an icy wind began to blow.
It blew great clouds from east to west
and pushed an egg out of a nest.

The egg rolled gently down a hill,
slow at first, then faster, until—

it bumped a rock and spun around
and came to land on level ground.

It sat there through that cold, dark night.
At last it felt the warm sunlight.
And with the light came thumping feet—
The lost egg called out, soft and sweet:

'Excuse me, please,
but am I yours?
I'm sure I am
a dinosaur's!'

First Stegosaurus wandered near
and asked the egg, loud and clear:

'What do you look like inside that shell?
I can't see in so I can't tell.
Are there spikes along your spine?
Long and flat and sharp like mine?'

'I have no spikes, I'm sad to say.
So I'm not yours, but that's okay.'

Next Brachiosaurus leaned in low
and asked his questions, calm and slow:

'What do you look like inside that shell?
I can't see in so I can't tell.
Do you have a longish neck?
Or is it short? Please can you check?'

'It's very short, this neck of mine.
So I'm not yours, but I'll be fine.'

Triceratops came trotting by
and spoke to the egg, eye to eye:

'What do you look like inside that shell?
I can't see in so I can't tell.
Do you have horns—one, two and three?
Three lovely sharp horns, just like me?'

'I have no horns—I wish I did—
so I'm not yours. I'm not your kid.'

Corythosaurus ambled past.
She stopped and stared, then spoke at last:

'What do you look like inside that shell?
I can't see in so I can't tell.
Is there a crest upon your head?
Or is it flat and smooth instead?'

'I have no crest (I just checked now)
so I'm not yours. Thanks, anyhow.'

Tyrannosaurus came to see
and asked the egg, quite lovingly:

'What do you look like inside that shell?
I can't see in so I can't tell.
Do you have a mouth of teeth?
Sharp up top and sharp beneath?'

'My teeth are few,' the egg replied.
'So I'm not yours,' it said, and sighed.

The sun sank slowly in the sky
and the lonely egg began to cry . . .

'The light of day is fading fast.
I'm sure this night will be my last!
I can't stay out in wind and storm!
I'll freeze alone! I must stay warm!'

'You are not ours, whose could you be?
We wish there was a way to see.'

But as the sun began to set,
it showed a perfect silhouette . . .

A pair of wings, a pointy snout.
And two strong legs, both short and stout.

'We see you now inside your shell!

We know your folks!

We know them well!'

The egg was rolled back up the hill,
rolled and nudged and pushed until
they reached a soft and sandy mound.
They left it where it would be found.

Then came the thump of heavy feet.
The egg called out, so soft and sweet . . .

'One last time—I must be sure—
Are you the ones I'm looking for?'

'We are. We are! We are YOURS!
We're two ECSTATIC pterosaurs.'

And when the night had come and gone
—the sky was clear, the bright sun shone—
there came a tap! A crack! A scratch!
And the lucky egg began to hatch.